Listen to That

written by Pam Holden
illustrated by Elise Smith

We can hear
the birds.

We can hear
the drums.

We can hear the water.

We can hear
the thunder.

We can hear
the dogs.

We can hear
the sirens.

We can hear
the bees.

We can hear
the pigs.
Grunt! Grunt!